Swamp Angel

Swamp Angel

by ANNE ISAACS

illustrated by

PAUL O. ZELINSKY

Dutton Children's Books

NEW YORK

Library of Congress Cataloging-in-Publication Data
Isaacs, Anne.
Swamp Angel/by Anne Isaacs;
illustrated by Paul O. Zelinsky.—1st ed.
p. cm.
Summary: Along with other amazing feats, Angelica Longrider, also
known as Swamp Angel, wrestles a huge bear, known as Thundering Tarnation,
to save the winter supplies of the settlers in Tennessee.
ISBN 0-525-45271-0
[1. Tall tales. 2. Frontier and pioneer life—Tennessee—
Fiction. 3. Tennessee—Fiction.]
I. Zelinsky, Paul O., ill.   II. Title.
PZ7.I762Sw   1994   [Fic]—dc20
93-43956   CIP   AC

Published in the United States 1994 by
Dutton Children's Books, a division of Penguin Books USA Inc.
375 Hudson Street, New York, New York 10014
Designed by Sara Reynolds and Paul O. Zelinsky
Printed in USA
First Edition
3 5 7 9 10 8 6 4

*The illustrations for this book were painted in oils
on cherry, maple, and birch veneers.*

For my mother
A.I.

For my wife, Deborah
P.O.Z.

On August 1, 1815, when Angelica Longrider took her first gulp of air on this earth, there was nothing about the baby to suggest that she would become the greatest woodswoman in Tennessee. The newborn was scarcely taller than her mother and couldn't climb a tree without help.

Although her father gave her a shiny new ax to play with in the cradle, like any good Tennessee father would, she was a full two years old before she built her first log cabin.

But by the time she was full grown, she was second to none in buckskin bravery, performing eye-popping wonders in the bogs and backwoods of Tennessee.

When she was twelve, a wagon train
got mired in Dejection Swamp. The settlers
had abandoned their covered wagons and nearly all
hope besides. Suddenly, a young woman in a homespun dress
tramped toward them out of the mists. She lifted those wagons
like they were twigs in a puddle and set them on high ground.
"It's an angel!" cried the gape-mouthed pioneers.

Ever since that time, Angelica Longrider has been known as Swamp Angel. To this day, stories about Swamp Angel spring up like sunflowers along the wagon trails. And every one of them is true.

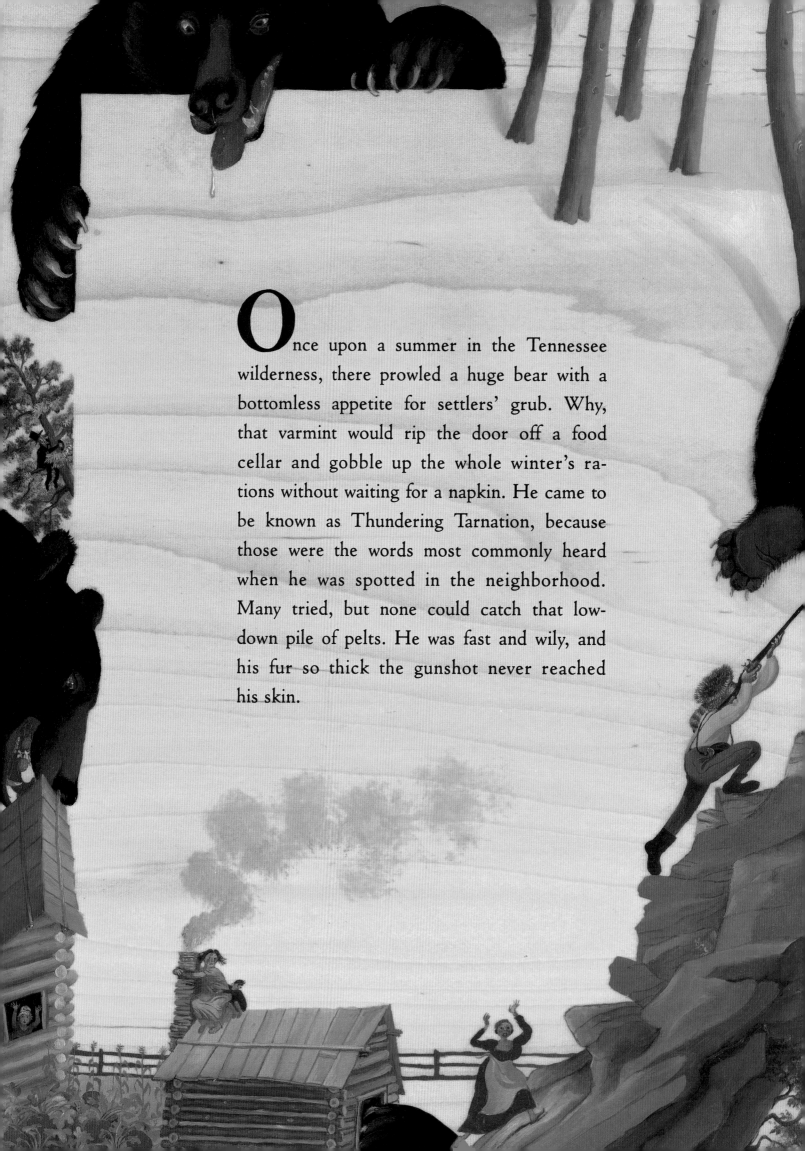

Once upon a summer in the Tennessee wilderness, there prowled a huge bear with a bottomless appetite for settlers' grub. Why, that varmint would rip the door off a food cellar and gobble up the whole winter's rations without waiting for a napkin. He came to be known as Thundering Tarnation, because those were the words most commonly heard when he was spotted in the neighborhood. Many tried, but none could catch that low-down pile of pelts. He was fast and wily, and his fur so thick the gunshot never reached his skin.

Before long, Thundering Tarnation had cleaned out half the root cellars in Tennessee. The settlers were desperate with no food to get them through the long winter ahead. So they sent word across the land of a competition to kill that bear. The reward for the successful hunter was to be Tarnation's enormous pelt, equal to a whole year's hunting and worth a lot more, on account of his fame. Beyond that, the winner would earn a powerful reputation, and the title of Champion Wildcat.

Now, it's well known, and a fact, too, that Tennessee daredevils are as plentiful as dewdrops on corn. Pretty soon, there was a long line of men in coonskin caps, waiting to sign up for the hunt. But when Swamp Angel stepped in line, one of those buckskins called out: "Hey, Angel! Shouldn't you be home, mending a quilt?"

Says she, "Quiltin' is men's work!"

"Well, how about baking a pie, Angel?"

"I aim to," says she. "A bear pie."

Their hoots and taunts didn't stop Swamp Angel from signing up and setting out to find that bear.

Tarnation left a pretty clear
trail. The first hunter
was found wearing an
empty molasses bucket,
a silly grin on his face.
Seems he'd tried the sweet
approach and got licked
in more ways
than one.

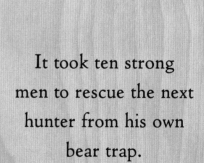

It took ten strong
men to rescue the next
hunter from his own
bear trap.

A third set out with
a hardened hickory
club and ended up
waist-deep in
toothpicks.

Another was discovered
wandering in circles,
clutching two fistfuls of fur.
His head was completely
bald, his beard mighty scarce.
Seems he'd traded pelts
with Thundering Tarnation
and got the worst
of the bargain.

Soon Swamp Angel was the only one left who hadn't met up with Tarnation. Until one morning she awoke from dozing in the shade of a creek to find that four-legged forest of stubble staring at her across the stream. They faced off for a few minutes. "Varmint," says Angel, "I'm much obliged for that pelt you're carryin'."

"*Grrrr,*" says Tarnation.

Then they waded into the stream and commenced to fight.

Swamp Angel took hold of that bear and tossed him so high he was still on the way up at nightfall. Even when the first star came out, there was no sign of him. Angel began to think she had lost him in the sky.

Now, Angel was bound and
determined to get Tarnation's pelt.
Just at that moment, a tornado
whirled by with a spout clear up
to the clouds. Swamp Angel
grabbed hold of it and swung
the twister around like a
giant lasso in the heavens.
She roped that bristled bandit
and brought him crashing
back to earth.

Locked in a bear hug, Swamp Angel and Thundering Tarnation wrestled across the hills of Tennessee. They stirred up so much dust that those hills are still called the Great Smoky Mountains. They fought three days and three nights without a break.

On the fourth day, they wrestled their way into a lake fifty feet deep. Tarnation pinned Angel to the muddy bottom with one of his gigantic paws.

To get a breath of air, she had to drink the whole lake dry.
"That was mighty refreshing," says Angel.

But it didn't look good for Angel, down in the muck under that mountain of mange. No matter how she struggled, she could not free herself from Tarnation's paw. Then Angel had an idea.

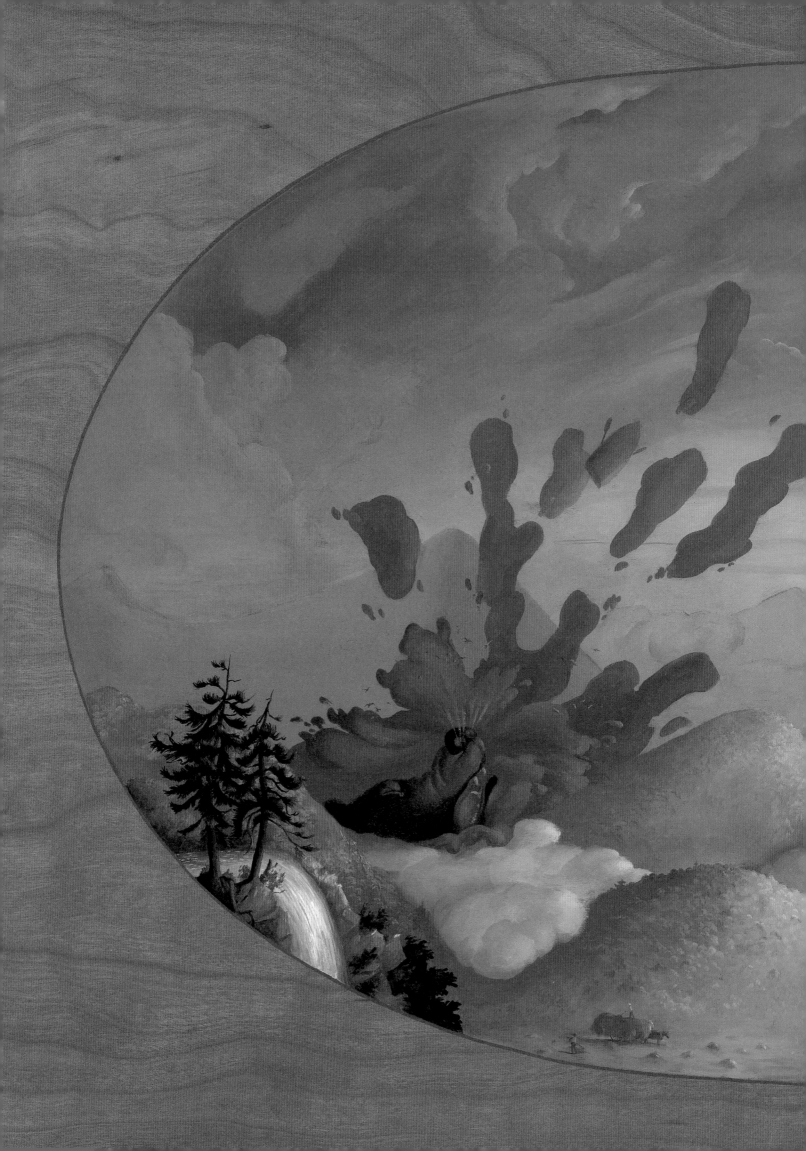

She opened her tobacco pouch and emptied it onto
the end of Tarnation's nose. He sniffed, threw back
his head, and sneezed so hard the mud flew off
the lake bottom, and Angel with it.

She hiked back ten miles from where she had landed, and the fight commenced once more.

Swamp Angel and Tarnation finally grew so tired they fell asleep, but that didn't stop them. They wrestled in their sleep.

Tarnation snored louder than a rockslide, while Angel snored like a locomotive in a thunderstorm. Their snoring rumbled through the earth, tumbling boulders and shaking trees loose. By morning, they had snored down nearly the whole forest.

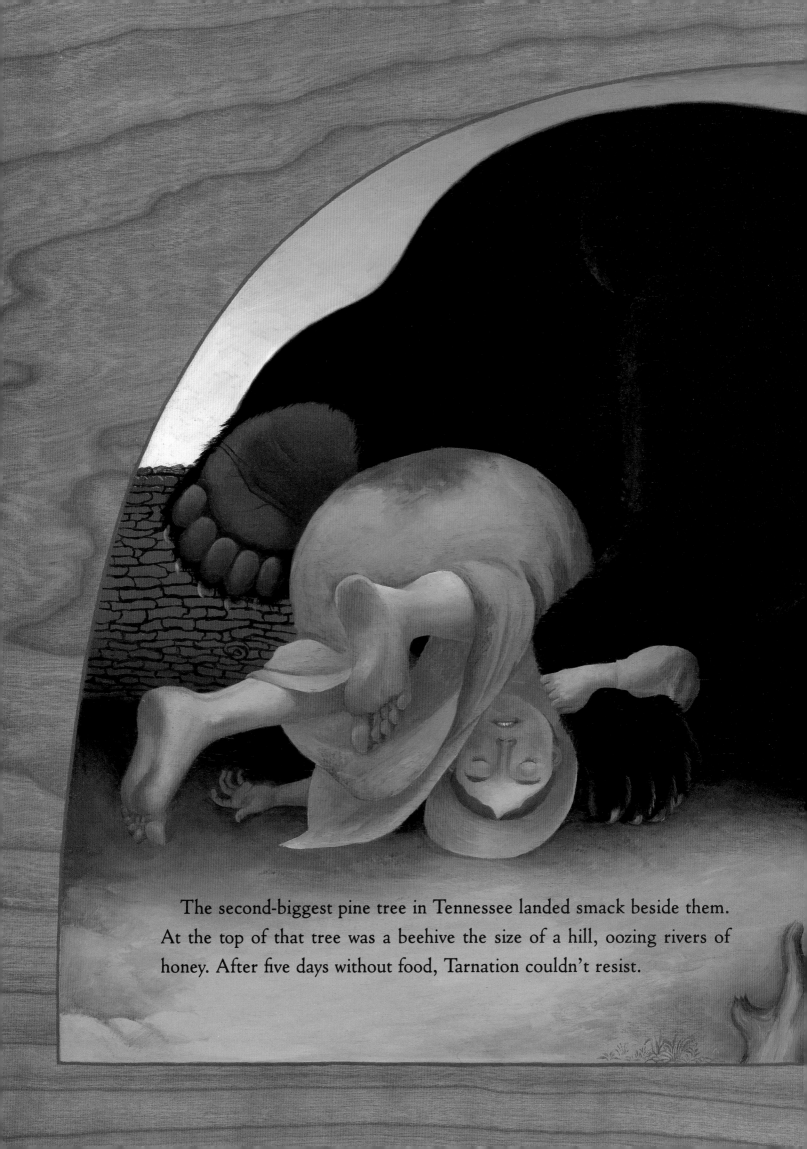

The second-biggest pine tree in Tennessee landed smack beside them. At the top of that tree was a beehive the size of a hill, oozing rivers of honey. After five days without food, Tarnation couldn't resist.

He rolled over in his sleep and sank his jaws into the sweet syrupy torrent. As he guzzled and slurped, Swamp Angel snored down one last tree.

It fell right on top of Thundering Tarnation. That bear was dead as a stump, and considerably flatter. When Angel awoke and saw what had happened, she plucked off her hat, bowed her head, and offered up these words of praise: "Confound it, varmint, if you warn't the most wondrous heap of trouble I ever come to grips with!"

That night, Tarnation fed everyone in Tennessee, I can tell you. It was the biggest celebration the state had ever known. There were bear steaks and bear cakes, bear muffins and bear stuffin', bear roast and bear toast. To wash it all down, there was berry wine. You could hear waist-coat buttons popping as far away as Kentucky. The leftovers filled all the empty storehouses in Tennessee, just before the first snowfall.

Swamp Angel decided to keep Thundering Tarnation's pelt as a rug. It was too big for Tennessee, so she moved to Montana and spread that bear rug out on the ground in front of her cabin. Nowadays, folks call it the Shortgrass Prairie.

Now, you may think no more was ever seen of
Thundering Tarnation, but that is not the case.
Back when Angel threw him up in the sky, he
crashed into a pile of stars, making a
lasting impression. You can still see
him there, any clear night.